The Secret Language Of Trees

Marie Skrobak

Marie Skrobak

Fulton Books, Inc.
Meadville, PA

First originally published by Fulton Books 2017

ISBN 978-1-63338-683-9 (Paperback)
ISBN 978-1-63338-684-6 (Digital)

Printed in the United States of America

Bill Sobeck was a very happy man.

He was a farmer and grew many things on his land.

The people in town loved him because he always wore a smile and gave them a cheerful hello.

They called him Farmer Bill.

Farmer Bill had many wonderful memories of growing up on his parents' farm.

One day, after he was all grown up, his father retired and gave the farm to him.

Now he was responsible for all the plants and animals living on that land.

Farmer Bill had many, many acres.

Some of Farmer Bill's land was covered in gardens and orchards.

He would go every week to the farmers market in town and sell what he had harvested.

He grew asparagus, tomatoes, cucumbers, and pumpkins.

He also grew broccoli, carrots, zucchini, and many other vegetables.

His orchards produced three kinds of apples, some apricots, and a few pears as well.

He even had some grapevines, but the summer wasn't long enough to provide many grapes.

Farmer Bill had many, many acres. Some of those acres were covered in meadow.

He and his dog, Doppler, loved to walk through the meadow every morning.

They saw grasses and wildflowers coming up in the spring.

They found bird's nests and rabbit holes in the summer.

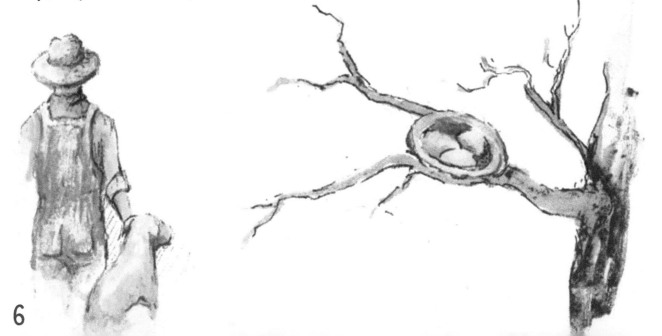

In fall, there were busy squirrels gathering food and white-tailed deer trying to fatten up for the cold winter.

And when winter came, the meadows were carpeted with a soft layer of snow whispering and shifting as the fierce winds blew.

The remaining acres of Farmer Bill's land were covered in trees.

One section had red pines, white pines, and a few spruce trees sprinkled in between.

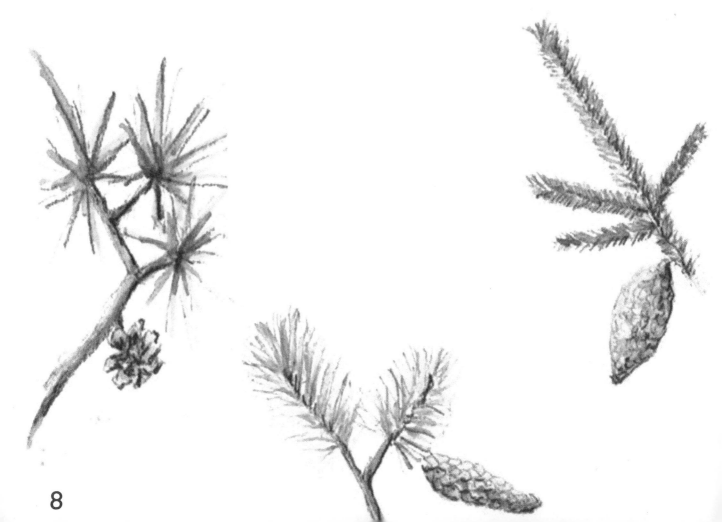

Much of those remaining acres were filled with hardwoods, such as beech-trees, ash trees, and ironwood.

But mostly, there were maple trees. Farmer Bill and Doppler enjoyed collecting sap from them each spring to make tasty maple syrup.

What Farmer Bill and all the townspeople didn't know was that these trees could talk!

They had their own language, so humans never knew what they were saying.

They could sigh, rattle, and click. They could creak, groan, and swoosh.

They made many other noises too.

Every year, when the holidays came, the trees had a Christmas party.

The pines wore beautiful, soft green clothing decorated with bird's nests and any pinecones they still had.

The hardwoods showed off their gorgeous bark topped with elegant branches and twigs.

They even had a few leaves hanging on here and there.

The problem was, the trees stayed in their own groups and just talked among themselves. They never got to know one another.

The hardwoods didn't know that the pines were friendly and helpful. They provided cover and protection for the birds and rabbits all year long.

And the pines didn't know the hardwoods were strong and could have many different looks.

They could sway in the strong wind without breaking and grew leaves that started out green in the spring and turned many different colors in autumn before falling off altogether.

Now, a few of the trees were getting tired of always being in their own group.

It seemed like they always talked about the same old things every year.

They wanted to have different conversations and learn new things.

The pines decided they would say hello to the hardwoods.

And the hardwoods thought maybe they would compliment the pines on their beautiful green color.

"Swish, moan, sigh," said the pine trees to the hardwoods.

"Creak, rattle, groan," said the hardwoods to the pines.

But the trees couldn't hear one another across the strip of meadow that ran between them.

*W*hatever shall we do?
wondered the hardwoods.

What if they think
we aren't friendly?
worried the pines.

Now, it just so happened that there was somebody else listening to all this.

Somebody that listened to everything all over Farmer Bill's land.

It was the wind!

The wind knew the hardwoods were strong and turned many different colors, and she knew the trees could all be friends if they could just talk to one another.

So the wind thought and thought until she came up with an idea.

"I'm pretty friendly myself," she said to the hardwoods. "And I certainly like to be helpful when I can," she said to the pines.

"I'll tell you what," she said to all of them. "Since I can move in any direction, I will carry the words of the hardwoods to the pines and then carry the answer of the pines back to the hardwoods."

Well, the trees all thought this was a very fine idea.

"We love your green Christmas apparel!" the wind carried to the pines.

"We love your holiday bark and elegant branches!" the wind carried back to the hardwoods. After that, they all started talking up a storm, and the wind was rushing every which way.

This would be the best Christmas party yet!

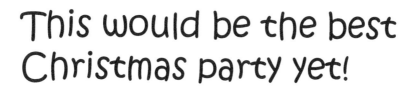

And of course, as Farmer Bill walked with Doppler through the swaying trees, all he saw was blowing snow.

And all he heard was *Whoosh, creak, sigh, rattle . . .*

"What a lovely, quiet Christmas Eve!" he said to Doppler as they headed home for dinner and a cozy evening by the fire.

ABOUT THE AUTHOR

Marie Skrobak grew up in a state park her father managed in Northern Michigan. This instilled in her a love of all things plant and animal. She got a business degree and later became a licensed veterinary technician, all the while fostering her love of writing (often creating silly poems and songs about her badly behaved pets). Marie has a home on three acres surrounded by trees and wildlife. This is her first published work.

CPSIA information can be obtained
at www.ICGtesting.com
Printed in the USA
BVHW02s2026300318
512130BV00001B/1/P